WORDTAMER QUI

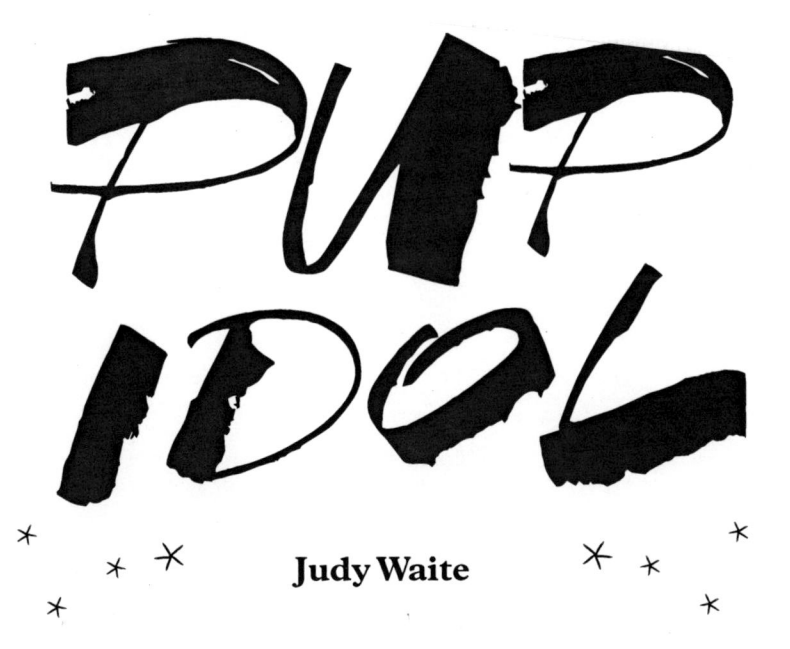

PUP IDOL

Judy Waite

The bag shuddered. The split in the side grew bigger. The rat's nose appeared. Then the rest of its face. Filthy. Black with mud. "You're massive. A giant rat," Jack said, not sure whether to be scared or impressed. But then Jack realised exactly what he was looking at. The creature struggling to get free wasn't a rat at all.

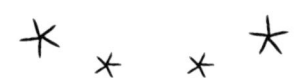

Copyright © Judy Waite 2014

The right of Judy Waite to be identified as the author of this work has been asserted by her in accordance with the Copyright, Designs and Patents Act 1988.

First published in Great Britain by Wordtamer Press
Wordtamer Press first edition published 2014

Set in Plantin by Alex Prior
Printed and bound in Great Britain by Lightning Source Milton Keynes

All rights reserved. No part of this publication may be reproduced, stored in a retrievals system, or transmitted, in any form or by any means, without the prior permission of the publisher.

Within the UK, exceptions are allowed in respect of any fair dealing for the purpose of research or private study, or criticism or review, as permitted under the Copyright, Designs and Patents Act 1988, or in the case of reprographic reproduction in accordance with the terms of the licences issued by the Copyright Licensing Agency. Enquiries concerning reproduction outside of these terms and in other countries should be sent to judywaite@aol.com, or via www.wordtamer.co.uk email link.

This book is sold subject to the condition that it shall not, by way of trade or otherwise, be lent, re-sold, hired out or otherwise circulated without the author's prior consent in any form of binding or cover other than that in which it is published and without a similar condition including this condition being imposed on the subsequent purchaser.

ISBN 978-0-9569832-2-0

WORDTAMER *QUICK WORDS* SERIES

PUP IDOL

Judy Waite

Go to the back of this book for ways to write a mystery story of your own, or visit:

www.wordtamer.co.uk

for extra story-writing tips and tricks.

For

Dan, Jessica, Lauren, Louie,
Tom and Thomas ... keep writing.
I'm proud of you all!

HUNGRY PUP

"Look at that puppy." Emily stopped so suddenly that Jack crashed into her. What was left of his burger slid out of the bun and onto the grass. A small brown and white puppy slunk out from behind the entrance to the Mirror Maze. It snatched the meat and ran under the carousel ride.

Emily dodged a gang of children who were scrambling up onto the brightly painted horses. She crouched down. "Look at its floppy ears. They're so cute."

Jack crouched next to Emily. The puppy looked out at them both with dark, hopeful eyes. "It nicked my food. I'm still hungry."

"Not as hungry as the pup. It's really skinny."

"Maybe it's got worms." Jack wasn't sure the puppy was hungrier than him. He wanted another burger, but Emily had paid for that last one. He couldn't let her do that again.

"That's a gross thing to say. Don't you like dogs?"

Jack crouched next to her. The carousel started up again; the funfair music so loud that he had to shout. "I was bitten by a dog when I was a kid. I've still got the scars." He waved his arm in front of Emily's nose. He was proud of the scar, and it came in useful when he wanted to look hard and cool.

Emily frowned. "A dog did that to you?"

"Yeah." Jack didn't add that the dog had actually been chasing a cat and knocked him off his bike. The scar came from the bike chain, but it looked a bit tooth-like. A dog attack sounded much better than a tumble from a bike.

"Well, this pup wouldn't hurt you." Emily clicked her fingers, throwing the remains of her own burger under the roundabout. "Here, puppy. D'you want more food?"

"You shouldn't encourage it. What happens if it follows us? You can't have a dog because you're about to go on holiday and pets aren't allowed at my place. I found that out when Mr Slither escaped just after I first moved in."

"A snake is hardly the same thing as a dog. That poor Miss Biddle next door to you must have almost had a heart attack when it came sliding out from her knicker drawer. On Christmas day, too. I'm not surprised your foster mum made you get rid of it."

"Mr Slither was a true mate. I've been harmed by the loss of him. I should have been offered help to get me through the trauma."

"That last bit's true. You definitely need help."

"Thanks for that."

Emily turned back to the puppy. "I don't go to Spain until just before we break up from school. That's nearly a week away. I could look after it for a few days, then put a card in the chip shop offering it free to a good home. It would be like getting it fostered."

"Leave it, Emily. Having it for a few days then letting it go is worse than never having it at all." Jack knew about staying in places for a few days, then getting moved on. He'd only been in his new home since just before Christmas. Sally Charm, his foster mum, was OK. The other three foster kids were a pain. "Anyway, what would you do if no one answered your ad? You'd be stuck with a puppy just as you were off to your luxury villa."

"You're right," Emily sighed. "It probably belongs to someone at the fair here anyway."

"How long are you going to Spain for?" Jack didn't like looking into the sad eyes of the puppy. He wanted to change the subject.

"The whole six weeks."

"Six weeks. Your own pool. Right next to the beach. I bet it's awesome."

"I wish we weren't going for so long. Plus, that talent contest is on towards the end of the summer. The winners of each town get to be in the telly final. Pixie Pink is one of the judges. She's amazing. Are you going to try for it with your guitar?"

"You joking? No way am I good enough." Mr Chung at school said he was making 'excellent progress' but playing guitar was harder than Jack had expected. "My dreams of super-stardom have taken a bit of a knock since I started learning. I'll have to find fame and fortune some other way. Anyway there was an article in the local paper about that contest. A parrot won last year. So they're looking for wacky stuff, not actual talent."

"I don't care about winning. It would just be so cool to sing in front of Pixie Pink." Emily sang a few lines from an old nursery rhyme Jack remembered from when he was still living with Dad. *With a nick nack paddywack, give a dog a bone, this old man came rolling home.*

The puppy wagged its tail uncertainly, as if it was getting braver.

Jack felt suddenly angry. He didn't want this puppy coming up to them. He didn't want to start to like it and care about it, and then have to walk away.

He stood up. "The fair moves on tomorrow, so we should look round it now." He made his voice light, to show Emily he'd forgotten about the puppy already. "I've got just enough money for one go on that duck-grab. I might win a fluffy teddy."

"You could give it to Miss Biddle as a way of saying sorry about the knicker-drawer drama." Emily stood up with him. "It might make her like you a bit more."

Jack could tell she was trying to have a light sort of voice too. "Don't hold your breath on that one."

They walked away from the puppy, almost crashing into a bearded man who had a skinny brown dog trotting beside him.

The dog started barking.

"Shut it, Trixie," growled the man, grabbing

the dog by the scruff of its neck. "Sorry, kids. She won't bite. Just nervous." The man made a clicking noise with his tongue and Trixie slunk beside him as he walked away.

"That man looked cruel. I feel so sorry for the dog. I bet she's had a tough life."

Jack didn't answer. He knew Emily thought he'd had a tough life too. Maybe she was only mates with him because she felt sorry for him? He was just another stray for her to rescue.

Jack got on with Emily better than he'd ever got on with anyone. He'd even been round to her house. It was a new place. For posh-toffs, his dad would have said. Her parents had been out and she'd forgotten her key, but she'd been OK about him seeing where the spare was kept. *'Under that rose bush by the patio doors. You get it for me, Jack. Roses are scratchy.'* Emily trusted him, and that made her extra special. He wanted her to think he was cool. Not pathetic, like that puppy.

Jack glanced behind him. The puppy was watching them go. Jack's heart gave a twist. Could they really just leave it all alone? He could feel his eyes stinging, although he never cried. He rubbed at his eyes.

"You OK?" said Emily.

"Yeah. Great." Jack turned back to her. "Just got a fly in my eye." He grabbed her arm and pulled her on through the funfair. Duck-Grab. Mirror Maze. Even that girly carousel. He didn't care what they went on, as long as it kept his mind off the puppy.

RAT CATCHER

A skinny brown dog streaked across the park. Its owner lumbered behind, shouting. Jack was too far away to work out what he was saying but he didn't sound happy. The dog crept back to him, its tail between its legs. Jack watched as they both headed for the gate that led to the back roads. He had been planning to head home that way, but he recognised the man. It was that beardy weirdy from the fair. Jack wasn't keen on going anywhere near him.

He turned to take the other path, then his heart sank. Holly and Lucas were mucking about by the bins. Jack couldn't stand Holly. Apart from anything else, she'd messed up his friendship with Lucas when she arrived at Sally's a few months before. Lucas did what she told him to do. It was usually bad stuff. And Jack was one of her favourite targets.

Jack wondered if perhaps the 'beardy weirdy' route might be safer after all, but there was something about that man that gave him goosebumps. It would be better to risk walking past Holly. It was the last day of school, so hopefully she'd be celebrating the start of six weeks of freedom and not be out to give him a hard time.

Jack wished Emily was with him, but Emily was already in Spain.

He shifted his school rucksack so it was more balanced, then headed towards them.

"Let's kick the ball in the bin." Holly stood with her hands on her hips. "Three goes each. Whoever wins gets to keep the ball."

"That ball belongs to Max," Lucas said. "I 'borrowed' it from under his bed."

"You'd better make sure you win then." Holly took the first kick. It bounced straight in the bin. "Sheer genius. Go get it, Lucas. Your turn now."

Jack saw Lucas peer inside. "Oh, gross! I'm not touching that."

"What's the problem?" Holly walked across and stood next to Lucas.

Jack watched as Lucas pointed inside the bin, his face twisted, like he was sucking lemons.

"*That's* the problem."

"Oh, cool. A rat." Holly giggled, but Jack noticed she stepped away. "You're not scared, are you?"

" 'Course not. But rats are disgusting. I don't want their filthy germs."

"Hey," Jack called, jogging the last few paces to join them. "I can sort this. I used to have rats as pets."

"This is no pet," said Holly. "This is probably Killer Rat. The deadliest rat in the world."

"I can at least take a look. My rats were trained. My dad taught me how to do it." Jack thought Holly would be impressed. Him and Dad had even made a video, and they'd put it out on you-tube. "Rats are smart. Mine were called Jerry and Jemima and …"

Holly poked him in the chest. "Shut up. You're annoying me."

"I just thought I could help."

"*I just thought I could help,*" Holly mimicked in a fake voice. "Nobody cares about your stupid dancing rats. Get lost."

"They didn't dance. They …"

"I don't care if they rode rockets to the moon. We don't give a stuff. OK?" Holly pushed her face close to Jack's.

"Leave him, Holly," said Lucas. "We don't want him telling Sally we gave him a hard time. I'll get a stick and hook the ball out. We'll play footie again."

"Forget the footie. I think we should give Jack a warning. A taste of what might happen if he opens his mouth."

"How?"

"I've just thought of a game that's way better than footie. It's called 'chase the loser'," said Holly.

"I don't need any warnings," Jack said, holding his hands up. "I'm not someone who blabs. I'm going."

"You're right. You *are* going. But we'll be behind you. We'll give you a head start. When I say 'go' you run for it. Then we'll count down from ten and start chasing. If you can get to the other end of that mesh fence before we catch you, you'll be safe. If not, we'll take you for a swimming lesson. In the ditch."

Jack looked across at the mesh fence that screened off a building site. It was at the furthest end of the park and he wasn't the greatest runner in the world. But he had to try. The ditch was disgusting. He didn't want to end up in there. "OK." He hoped his voice wasn't as shaky as his legs. "Ready when you are."

He straightened up.

Holly straightened up too. "On your marks, get set, GO!"

Jack ran.

Behind him, he heard Lucas counting, leaving long gaps between each number. "Ten – nine – eight – seven – six ..."

Then Holly joined in, counting faster. She said the last three numbers so fast, the words were blurred. "Five – four – threetwoone." Then she gave a wild whoop. "Here we come, loser."

Jack ran so fast his legs hurt.

Behind him, their footsteps pounded closer. Holly drew level with him. "Oh no, look at this, Lucas." She was yelling in Jack's ear as she grabbed his elbow. "Poor Jack's falling over. He's rolling towards the ditch."

Holly bumped and pushed Jack into the ditch. Holly was strong, but even if she hadn't been, Jack knew better than to put up a fight. He let himself fall. The stinking water oozed round him. It soaked his school uniform. It trickled inside his shirt.

"Crazy place to go swimming." Holly peered down at him. "Don't you know it's full of toxins in there? You could catch a dreadful disease." She grinned, then turned to Lucas. "I'm bored. Let's head to the building site and annoy that fat security guy. We can make his psycho dog go crazy again."

Lucas wouldn't look at Jack. He stared down at the grass. "Yeah. Cool. Let's go."

Jack waited. He'd get out when they were gone. If Holly turned round and saw him back on dry land, she might come and shove him in again.

There was a supermarket trolley in the ditch, and a filthy plastic bag lay in the middle. It looked full of dead leaves and mud. Someone had knotted it at the top. He gripped the trolley handle, using it to steady himself. The trolley shifted, its wheels sinking deeper in the squelch. Just at that moment, the bag of muck moved. It squirmed. Jack stared in horror. Were the toxins coming to life? Had the chemicals clashed together and formed some sort of muck-monster? And then he realised. "I bet it's another rat," he said out loud. "It's gone sniffing in there and now it can't get out."

Jack knew it wasn't a good idea to open the bag with his hands. Rats had long, yellow teeth, and this one would be scared. But he had to let it out.

The cousins of this one had been his pets once. He grabbed a stick and poked it into the side of the bag.

It split straight away. Disgusting water leaked out. "Come on then, mate. You're free now. Best I can do for you."

Jack backed away as he spoke. The rat might attack him. "Come on, I won't hurt you." Jack made a clicking noise with his tongue, the way he'd done when he'd trained Jerry and Jemima.

The noise seemed to work.

The bag shuddered. The split in the side grew bigger. The rat's nose appeared. Then the rest of its face. Filthy. Black with mud. "You're massive. A giant rat," Jack said, not sure whether to be scared or impressed. But then Jack realised exactly what he was looking at. The creature struggling to get free wasn't a rat at all.

It was the puppy from the funfair.

BOG ROLL BURGLAR

Sally was talking to Miss Biddle across the front-garden fence. "I'm so sorry," she was saying. "I'll try and make sure they keep the noise down in the mornings. I'm fostering four at the moment, and none of them are the quiet type."

Jack guessed Miss Biddle was moaning about the noise again. But it was good that Sally was busy talking. She barely looked round as Jack squelched up the drive, went through the gate, and headed round the back of the house.

Moments later, he was in the downstairs bathroom and the puppy was huddled in the empty bath. "I can't keep you. You know that, don't you?"

The puppy looked up at Jack. Its eyes were big, and scared.

"Even if I was allowed to, I'm not really a doggie

person. I'm more into snakes and lizards. Things that look after themselves. But what's been done to you is just wrong. Whoever did it must be some sort of psycho."

Jack peeled off his dirty clothes, right down to his boxer shorts. "Sorry about this strip show, but I stink. Same as you do. I've got my PE kit in my rucksack, so once I've cleaned you up, I'll stick that on. Then I'll decide what to do."

Jack ran warm water from the taps and swilled it over the puppy.

The mud ran in puddles, and Jack reached for Sally's super-saver bubble bath. "You're really skinny. When's the last time you ate?"

The puppy shivered and Jack got worried that it was ill. It might die on him. Maybe it would have been better to have left it in that bag after all? It was clearly terrified of him. At least in that bag it would have died in peace.

And then he thought how stupid he was being. How could anything ever want to end its life in a plastic bag. Jack felt his eyes sting at the thought. "Must be this bubble-bath stuff getting in my eyes," he muttered to the puppy, as he rubbed the soap into its fur.

The puppy was still shivering, but now it was like a creature made of bubbles with two dark eyes staring out. Jack tried not to look into those eyes as he rinsed the soap off, then wrapped the puppy in a towel.

There was a hammering on the bathroom door. "Hey, who's in there? How long you gonna be?" It was Max. The youngest foster kid.

Jack had to think quickly. "I've got gut ache. Might be a while."

"Yuck. Hope you're not gonna stink the place out. Shall I get Sally?"

"No. No. It's OK. I'm nearly better. Just give me a few more minutes."

"Oh, gross. Way too much information. I'm going before the fumes hit me."

Jack listened to Max's footsteps as he walked away. Max was cute but he had the memory of a bean. Hopefully he'd use the upstairs loo and have forgotten all about Jack by the time he came out.

Jack didn't know what to do with the puppy, but he didn't want Sally to decide for him. It would be carted off to the dogs' home before you could say 'nick nack paddywack.' Sally was always getting complaints about noise, or mess, or problems with her foster children. She had a heart of gold, but Jack knew she wouldn't risk a puppy in the house. But Jack didn't want the puppy put in a dogs' home. A dogs' home was the same as a foster home.

He looked round. The window was open. He'd get outside and find somewhere to sit and think. Pulling on his PE kit, he rolled his stinky school uniform in a ball and stuffed it into his rucksack.

Keeping the puppy in the towel, he lowered that in too. "I'm going to have to zip you up, but I'll leave a gap so you can breathe."

Tiptoeing to the bathroom door, he unlocked it, just in case Sally did come to check up on him. Then, scrambling onto the window ledge, he lifted his rucksack and jumped out the open window onto the path.

"What you doing, Jack Jones?" Holly stood staring at him, the water bottle she'd been about to drink from held in mid-air. "You some secret bog roll burglar or something?"

There was no way Jack could risk letting Holly know what was in his rucksack. Holly was the sort of girl who would rip wings off flies and laugh. He didn't want to think what she might do to the puppy.

SOMEWHERE SECRET

"I'm – um – Max was after me. I'm trying to escape from him."

"How come you're wearing your PE kit, loser? And if it's not bog roll, what have you *really* got stashed in there?" Holly made a grab for the rucksack, but Jack dodged out of the way. "Mmm, interesting. You really don't want me to look, do you? Which means I want to know even more." Holly grabbed at it again.

Jack dodged the other way. "Trust me. You don't want to look. It's gross."

"What is?"

Jack hadn't been sure what he was going to say, but suddenly a brainwave moment zapped through him. Opening the zip just a tiny bit more, he pulled out one leg of his filthy school trousers.

"I got pushed in a ditch on the way home from school. If Sally saw my clothes, she'd want to know what happened. And you know how good she is at getting the truth out of us all."

Holly pretended to glare at Jack, but he could see she was worried.

At that moment, Sally herself came round the corner. "Holly? Jack? Are you two up to something? And why are you in your PE kit, Jack?"

Holly widened her eyes, looking as innocent as an angel. "Jack's just off to do some sports training. I was giving him some tips."

"Sport? That's not like you Jack."

"I'm going to practice running," Jack widened his own eyes. "I was rubbish at sports day. I thought the holidays would be a good time to get better."

"And I was just giving Jack my water bottle. I never used it today 'cos Mrs Tucker gave us all a picnic on the field." Holly held her bottle out to Jack.

"Most generous." Jack gave Holly a fake smile, and took the bottle.

"That's *lovely*, Holly. And excellent, Jack. Even if you don't make it to the next Olympics, keeping fit for the summer is a wonderful way to spend your time. Although …" she sniffed the air, and looked at Jack's PE shirt, "... it might be a good idea to let me give that a wash before you wear it again." She beamed at them both as if their new-found friendship gave her a reason for living, then walked away into the house.

Holly snapped back into glaring again. "Enjoy your workout," she growled. Then she followed on behind Sally.

Jack looked around the garden for somewhere to take the puppy. Sally kept the place tidy. There was nowhere to hide it. They had a garage, but he'd need to ask Sally for the key. He didn't want to risk any questions.

He looked over the fence into Miss Biddle's garden. It looked promising. Overgrown. Full of tangled bushes. Jack was good at climbing fences. And walls too, for that matter. He hadn't been that happy at some of his foster homes, or some of his other schools. Scrabbling over walls and fences had been part of everyday life for a while.

Jack scrambled across the fence. And then he saw the perfect place: an old shed, tucked away behind ivy and brambles.

Jack could put the puppy in there until he'd worked out what to do.

RIP

The shed was dark and dusty. A shaft of light from the window showed up cobwebs as thick as curtains. There was an old lawn mower. Some rusted tins of paint.

Jack put Holly's bottle down next to the paint tins. He found a blanket and opened it out. Then, unzipping his rucksack, he lifted the puppy out.

It still had the damp towel round it, but its eyes were tight shut. Its body was limp. Jack's heart gave a bounce, as if it had missed a beat. The puppy was dead.

He rocked the soft body in his arms. "Sorry, sorry, sorry," he whispered. "I messed up. I should've handed you in to Sally. The dogs' home would have looked after you better than me, after all."

Jack never cried, but dust seemed to be stinging his eyes. He wiped them with the back of his hand. "I'll bury you properly," he sniffed. "I'll dig you a hole, just like my dad did when Jemima died. There's got to be a spade in here somewhere."

He lay the puppy on the blanket. Then he got up and began looking for a spade. "This'll do." He lifted a trowel from one of the shelves, then, with one last glance at the lifeless body, he crept into the garden. There was an ache in his heart. The same sort of ache he used to get when he watched Dad drive away after his weekend visits. Jack hadn't felt that ache for ages. But then, he hadn't seen Dad in ages either. And anyway, he'd trained himself not to feel stuff like that. You didn't get anywhere by feeling sorry for yourself.

From upstairs in his own house, he could hear music booming out from Holly's bedroom. Lucas and Max were arguing about something in the kitchen. Miss Biddle would be round complaining again soon. Sally hadn't done much of a job keeping everyone quiet.

Jack stumbled over a stack of mossy stones and discovered an old pond grown over with weeds. He thought the soil would probably be easy to dig.

And then he saw a face in the bushes. He jumped backwards, scratching his legs on brambles. Then he sighed with relief. It was a stone mermaid. The face was covered in slime and bird poop, but it had a calm, kind expression. He'd bury the puppy beside it.

Jack worked hard at digging the hole. He was going to do the right thing for this puppy even though it was in doggy-heaven. It was his way to show it that he'd cared.

At last it seemed deep enough. The puppy wasn't very big, after all.

He found a stick and wrote across the mermaid's forehead in mud:

RIP

It meant 'rest in peace'. They'd written that for Jemima too. Jerry escaped not long after Jemima died, so Jack hadn't been able to do that for him. He stepped back, about to head to the shed for the puppy's body, when his foot brushed something. The something moved. Jack lost his footing and almost fell. Looking down, he saw what he'd tripped over. The puppy was sitting on its hind legs, as if it was begging. It had Holly's water bottle in its mouth.

"You didn't die, after all," said Jack.

The puppy whined and wagged its stumpy brown tail.

Jack knelt on the boggy ground and took the bottle. "You're thirsty, eh? I'll sort something. But I do have to put you back in the shed. I need to keep you very, very secret."

He glanced up towards Miss Biddle's house.

The afternoon sun glinted on the upstairs windowpane and, for a moment, he thought he saw someone move past, but it was just the reflection of a tree branch swaying in the light breeze. Still, the movement had got his heart racing. He had to get himself, and the puppy, out of sight.

Dog's Dinner

Sally walked through the kitchen with an armful of washing. "Jack, stop looking in that fridge. Where's your school uniform? I need to get it washed."

"Um. Er. Might have left it at school." Jack scanned the fridge for anything doggish. "We got any of that cold meat left?"

"No, we haven't. Why are you boys always so hungry? You'd eat me out of house and home if you got the chance. What do you mean, you left your uniform at school?"

"I changed into my PE kit, remember?" Jack glanced sideways at Holly, who was painting her nails at the table.

Sally frowned. "I thought you did that when you got home."

"I – um. No. Did it at school."

"It's true." Holly looked up with her angel eyes. "I saw Jack in the park and he definitely had his PE kit on then."

Sally sighed. "We'll have to ring school in the morning. I'm not sure if the office opens in the summer holidays, but if we don't get it soon the thing will get so disgusting it'll be able to walk here by itself."

"You saying my clothes have got bugs?" Jack didn't really care what Sally meant, but he needed to distract her while he carried on hunting through the fridge. Cheese? Bread? The truth about the school uniform was that he'd dumped it behind Miss Biddle's shed. It would rot away among the dead leaves and grass. He'd probably end up having to wear one of Lucas's hand-me-downs next term, which wouldn't be cool, but right now he had bigger things to worry about.

Sally bent down in front of the washing machine, pushing the clothes inside. Holly began sticking sequins onto her nails. Jack grabbed the cheese and stuffed it in his pocket. He poured himself a mug of milk.

"You're going to drink milk? Straight off?" Holly made a show of putting her fingers down her throat and faking a vomit noise. "Gross."

"It's part of my training plan, for my bodybuilding."

"Oh yeah, that." Holly checked to see that Sally wasn't looking, then stuck her tongue out at him.

Jack drank a mouthful of milk. Holly was right. It even smelt like someone had honked it up. But the plan was to take it to the shed.

Hurrying into the downstairs bathroom, he poured the milk into Holly's bottle. It leaked a bit because the puppy's teeth had punctured a hole in the plastic, so he wound bog roll round it to plug it up.

He went back to the kitchen. "I'm going out."

"Where to?" Sally was stacking the dishwasher.

"Just to hang about."

"Hanging about gets boys your age into trouble. Haven't you got a book to read, or something?"

"A *book*? You know I don't read books."

"If you don't read books, then how do you learn anything apart from what school teaches you?"

Jack shrugged. "Internet."

"Do that then," said Sally. "Go and google something. The distance from Mars to the sun. Or what makes the tide turn."

"How can anything like that be useful?" moaned Jack. "And anyway, Lucas is hogging the computer. *Please* let me go out, Sally. I need to train."

"You were training before dinner. You've done enough for one day. But if you're really keen on keeping fit we could all go swimming tomorrow." She beamed round at Holly, then back to Jack again.

"I'm not going swimming," muttered Holly, screwing the top back on her nail varnish. "I'm not playing happy families with anyone here."

Jack was struck by another brainwave. "I'll sit in the garden and look for stars. I'll take paper and draw what bit of the sky they're in, and google them later. I could learn about every star by the end of the holiday."

"How lucky I am," Holly yawned. "I've had the good fortune to end up in a foster home with a total geek."

"A geek with olympic potential," Jack said.

Sally was beaming more brightly than ever. "Stargazing is a lovely idea, Jack. It won't be dark for a little while, but I know some stars come out while it's still light."

Five minutes later Jack was out in the garden. Sally's notebook and pen were in his pocket, along with the cheese. He hoped Sally would be too busy to come and see how he was getting on.

Heading to the fence, he climbed over, crouching for a moment to check that Miss Biddle wasn't outside. There was no sign of her. Jack crept to the shed. He felt good about having a hidden puppy. Good about helping it. For the first time since he'd started being fostered, Jack felt as if he mattered.

The door opened with a creak.

Jack had half hoped the puppy would bound up to him, like a dog in a film. The shed stayed silent. Jack looked around. "Hey, puppy," whispered Jack. "I'm back. Cheese and milk."

Nothing.

The blanket was still on the floor. The damp towel hung from the top of a broom handle. There was the faint pong of poop. "Come on, poopy puppy," Jack called a bit louder. "Food time."

Still nothing.

Jack squinted at the boxes and cans stacked along the walls of the shed. Could the puppy have crept behind them? He lifted a box from a pile of books. The pile wobbled. Everything could come crashing down. The puppy might get squashed before he found it. "Just take it slowly," Jack whispered to himself. "Best not to rush."

He shifted books. Clothes. Flower pots. There were mouldy cushions and cans of paint. He jumped back from a spider with a body the size of a golf ball. But there was no puppy.

Jack ran his hand backwards through his hair. Maybe there was a hole somewhere? The puppy might have escaped. He felt sick thinking about what could happen. A fox might feast on it. It might drown in that pond. It could get squashed on the road.

Just then, Jack heard a noise behind him. A shadow darkened the doorway. For one terrifying moment, Jack forgot to breathe.

Miss Biddle stood with her arms folded. "Are you looking for something?" she croaked.

Stars in Their Eyes

"I used to train dogs, years ago." Miss Biddle, who was now insisting Jack called her 'Biddy' – she said it had been her nickname at school – was sat in a chair in her front room. "When I heard the yelping in the shed, it was a sound I knew. As soon as I found the little fellow, I guessed it would be something to do with one of you lot. I was looking out for you."

"I thought you'd be angry." Jack sat opposite her with the puppy on his lap. It was fast asleep, but every now and then it gave a little whimper, as if it were dreaming.

"I'd have a dog here if I could, but as you know, we're not allowed pets in these houses."

Jack wondered if this was a good time to apologise for the whole knicker-drawer drama, but he was getting on with her OK. He didn't want to spoil things.

He'd never been in her house before. It was all flowery and old lady-ish, but Jack liked it more than the easy-wipe walls and sensible brown carpets that Sally had.

"My dogs were stars." Biddy's eyes grew misty. "We trained them for film and television. They walked on their hind legs. Danced. Even sang."

"Sang?" Jack looked down at the puppy and stroked his ears. "How does a dog sing?"

"They learn to make sounds by certain triggers. Some dogs find it easier than others, so we had to test to find those that had a talent for it. Not all dogs can sing. Just the same as humans."

"My friend Emily can sing."

Biddy smiled. "Do you have a gift with anything?"

Jack wondered about saying he was having guitar lessons and that Mr Chung said he was doing well, but it sounded a bit big-headed. "Nah. Nothing."

"I never had anything I was special at either. Other than working with dogs, of course. Where does Sally think you are?"

"Sitting in the garden, drawing the stars."

"Do you think you should go back?"

Jack hesitated. "Are you going to take the puppy to a dogs' home?"

Now it was Biddy's turn to hesitate. "He needs somewhere permanent, fairly quickly. Puppies are like children. They need a safe, steady place to grow up in." She looked at Jack and suddenly seemed to realise what she'd said. "Not that I think your life next door isn't safe, or steady. But I'm sure it's tough sometimes. It's got to be harder than having a more everyday sort of home."

"Maybe." Jack shrugged and changed the subject back to the puppy again. "What if you just looked after him for a few days? I'd help. We could feed him up, then put a card in the chip shop offering him free to a good home? Emily wanted to do that, but she couldn't because she was going away."

Biddy rubbed her chin with her hand.

"You could even train him a bit," said Jack. "He's more likely to find a good home if he's learnt not to widdle on the carpet."

Biddy looked thoughtful.

"*Please* Miss Biddle. Er – Biddy. It's the summer

holidays so I can help too." Jack felt buzzed up. This was a genius solution. "Summer lasts for six weeks so that's masses of time to get him the best owner we can find."

Biddy sighed. "I'll decide in the morning. But you'd better give him to me now. You need to get back to Sally, before she sends out a search party."

Jack stood up and handed the puppy over to her. Straight away, he missed the warm feeling of it in his arms. He missed its sweet puppy smell.

"By the way," said Biddy, "what would you like to call him?"

Jack paused. "It feels wrong to name something I can't keep. It would be like saying it was mine – and then giving up on it." Jack shrugged. He knew he wasn't explaining himself very well, but how could he tell her that he was scared of caring too much for the puppy. He was scared of the sadness he'd feel when the new owner came for him.

"The little chap still needs a name," Biddy said gently. "If we're going to train him, he'll need a sound he can answer to."

Jack remembered Emily's song again. The one from when he was little. *With a nick nack paddywack give a dog a bone, this old man came rolling home.*

"How about Paddywack?" he said.

"Paddywack it is, then," said Biddy, humming the beginning of the song.

As if he had heard and understood, Paddywack gave a sharp little bark.

"Sounds like he approves," smiled Biddy.

Jack thought about the warm feeling and the puppy smell and he knew it didn't matter whether the puppy had a name or not. It was already too late. He was already going to be sad when the puppy went to his new home. But as he hurried across the garden, all Jack could think was that if he and Biddy trained the puppy really well, then someone special might want him.

Knowing Paddywack was with someone special was more important than his own stupid sadness.

THE MUSIC MAN

"I'm very proud of you," Sally told Jack over breakfast a few days later. "You're so kind, helping Miss Biddle with all those jobs."

Jack shrugged. "Just doing bits of stuff. The things she finds hard."

"Well, I think it's wonderful. And you're helping all of us here too. Miss Biddle hasn't complained about us once since the holiday started."

Jack wished Sally would back off. Paddywack's training was going well, but he didn't feel great about lying. And he felt even worse about the way she was painting him like some kind of saint.

"I don't get why Jack's being such a creep." Holly sat in her dressing gown, nibbling round the edges of a piece of toast. She turned to Jack. "You hoping she might leave you her life's savings if she pegs out?"

Sally's eyes widened. "Holly! That's a terrible thing to say."

"It's not like Jack's ever showed an interest in her before."

"Jack's always kind to me," said Max. "I like him."

"Everyone's kind to you," Holly sneered. "It's because you've got a bean-brain. They feel sorry for you."

"That's enough, Holly!" Sally shook her head and gave Max a hug. "Don't take any notice. Teenage girls can get tetchy sometimes."

Lucas smeared marmite onto a hunk of bread. "What exactly do you do round there?"

Jack kept his eyes fixed on his cornflakes. "We just talk mostly," he mumbled. "And I help her sort a few things out."

"What could someone like Miss Biddle want with talking to you?" Holly turned to Sally. "I bet he's up to something bad."

"I'm not up to *anything* bad." Jack pushed his dish away in a sudden display of anger. The last thing he wanted was for Sally to start 'popping round' to see how it was all going. "I'd just rather talk to her than any of you lot. Emily's away for the whole summer, so I'm filling in time. That's all." He turned to Sally. "I'm sorry if that's a wrong reason, but it's true. Or at least, that's how it started. But now I've got to know her we get on OK. I'm gonna take my guitar round there today. She said she wanted to hear me play." Jack hadn't planned to do anything of the sort, but as soon as he said it, it seemed like another genius idea. Sally had been on at him the night before, saying he needed to practise even though he wasn't having lessons for six weeks. If she thought he was going to play to Biddy, maybe she'd leave him alone.

"This gets worse and worse." Holly rolled her eyes. "Sing-along-with-Jack."

"Get lost."

"Shhh, Jack. Don't get upset. I think Holly's just got out the wrong side of the bed this morning. I'm sure Miss Biddle will love to hear you play."

"I didn't get out the wrong side of the bed. But if you're going to make all this my fault then I'm going BACK to bed." Holly did a dramatic show of flinging her toast down, tossing her hair and storming out of the room.

Lucas watched her go and Jack could see he was trying to decide whether to follow her or not. Max ate what was left of Holly's toast.

Jack stared down at the table. Everyone he lived with was rotten in their own way. He felt his eyes start to sting and he stood up quickly. "I'm going next door. This place is doing my head in."

"Don't forget to clean your teeth first." Sally smiled. "And don't let all this squabbling upset you. You've got a long summer ahead and you know the arguments always settle down in the end."

Ten minutes later Jack was round at Biddy's and Paddywack was chewing the laces on his trainers.

"You've brought your guitar?" Biddy looked puzzled.

"No one got why I keep coming to see you, so I made out you were interested in hearing me play."

"Well, I am. I'm very interested."

"I haven't been learning it long."

"Doesn't matter. It was clever of you to think of it. When you go home you can say I begged you to bring it again, and you can say the quiet here helps you concentrate."

Paddywack gave a small bark and looked up at Jack. "Sorry, Pads, aren't I paying you enough attention?" Jack picked the puppy up. "You're heavier already. A bit of a porky-pie."

"His tummy's full of chicken pieces and my best shoes," smiled Biddy. "But he's learning fast. Last night I trained him to sit and stay. He's a smart boy." Biddy glanced out the window. "Oooh look, Sally's outside in your back garden now. I'll open the kitchen door so she can hear you easily, and you get that guitar warmed up, or whatever needs to happen to it. I know quite a lot about singing, but I'm afraid I don't know much about instruments."

Jack got his guitar out of its case. He sat on a chair and strummed a few chords. Biddy fussed around in the kitchen making cakes and drinks.

Paddywack rolled on the floor and chewed the corner of the case.

"D'you want to learn music, Pads? These are the chords." Jack played a 'C' and a 'D'. Paddywack barked and wagged his tail.

"This is a scale." Jack plucked the strings more carefully.

From the kitchen, Biddy sang in a croaky old-lady voice, "Doe – ray – me."

Paddywack bounced inside Jack's guitar case, looked up and barked three times.

Biddy came back into the room. "Do that again, Jack. That scale."

Jack repeated the scale. Biddy sang again, this time holding the third sound for longer. "Doe – ray – meeee."

Paddywack barked twice, and then howled.

Biddy hurried to close the window. She pulled a chair up next to Jack. "Do it again, slower."

Jack played slowly.

Biddy sang slowly.

Paddywack barked slowly.

"Now faster."

Jack strummed faster. Biddy sang faster. Paddywack did three fast barks.

"You know what we've got here, don't you, Jack?"

"A dog that's into guitars?"

"More than that. A singing dog." Biddy smiled and her eyes were shining. "In all my time as a trainer, I've never known a dog to pick up a tune this quickly. And he's so young. If we could develop that talent, he could be incredible." Then her smile faded. "Except, of course, we're not supposed to have him. How on earth could we get people to see how talented he is?"

Jack was quiet for a moment, then he said, "There's this talent show coming up. The winners get to be on telly. A parrot won last year, so it must be OK to enter animals."

Biddy rubbed her chin. "If he's good enough to get to the television final, his future will be safe. People will be fighting to give him a home."

Jack strummed his guitar again and sang softly, "This old man, he played one, he played nick nack on my thumb. With a nick nack paddywack give a dog a bone, this old man came rolling home."

Paddywack scrambled onto the chair beside him, yelping in time to the music.

STAGE FRIGHT

The next morning Jack knelt in Biddy's kitchen. "Me and my dad trained rats once." Paddywack rolled onto his back. Jack tickled his pink-puppy tummy. "My girl rat, Jemima, learnt to blow kisses and wave goodbye. And Jerry could actually stick a ball in a net. A little plastic ball, it was. Dad made the net for me."

Biddy looked round from the cake she was mixing. "Did you give them treats to help them learn?"

"They got cereal, and bits of fruit and stuff. Dad said it was important we didn't feed them anything bad."

"Your dad was right. A fat rat would be sad to see, however clever it was." Biddy went over to the kitchen drawer. "I bought this yesterday. It's a clicker. Dogs like the sound of it, and we click it whenever Paddywack gets something right. We can start by offering rewards of food, just like you did with your rats, but I don't think he'll need treats for long."

"It's not cruel, is it? Training him to sing?"

"I did sometimes come across cruel trainers – one man used to starve his dogs so they'd be more desperate for the treats, but I always found dogs learnt because they wanted to do things well. They enjoyed it."

Jack picked Paddywack up and hugged him tightly. The puppy licked his nose. Jack felt worried. There were people in the world who would starve a dog. Were they the same sorts of people who'd put one in a bag and dump it in a ditch? How could he be really, *really* sure that Paddywack would find a good home?

Biddy popped her cake in the oven and smiled at Jack. "Right, that's the treat for us humans sorted. Shall we go through to the other room and start today's training?"

Jack sat down and got his guitar ready. He did the chords first. Then the scales. Then he played a mash of notes he made up as he went along.

Biddy clicked her clicker. Paddywack howled happily. The warm scent of baking wafted in from the kitchen.

Jack knew he should be pleased, but there was something wrong. He put the guitar down suddenly. "This talent show. How are we going to do it? Are we going to take a recording of me playing, or something?"

"Oh no, you'll need to be with him. You'll need to perform too."

"Me!?" Jack nearly fell off the chair. "I can't. I'd mess it up. I was in a school nativity once and I dropped the baby Jesus doll on its head."

"Paddywack will need you to be there. The bond between the two of you is part of the act."

"But my guitar playing is rubbish."

Biddy stroked Paddywack's ears "You sound fine to me."

"Fine? 'Fine' is boring. Pads needs to be matched with someone as awesome as he is. Not a Grade One beginner."

"Well, you're one grade better at it than I am. And we don't have any other options. I used to sing to the dogs I trained, but I'm too croaky now. I'd get booed off stage."

Jack's gut lurched with a new panic. "Will the audience really boo people?"

"Now, stop worrying. This is only the first day. We've got a whole five weeks to get this right."

But Jack *was* worrying. He worried for the rest of the morning. He worried that afternoon when he was googling the talent show on the computer. He worried that evening when he sat in the bedroom he shared with Max. He got his guitar out and played 'doe-ray-me' again. He made up a new mash of notes.

Holly appeared in the doorway. "Get me some earplugs. If that's the rubbish you're playing to old Biddle next door, then firstly she must be deaf. Secondly, be short on brain cells. And thirdly ..." she looked around the bedroom, then shrugged. "Actually, I can't think of a third one. But basically, she must be completely insane."

She stormed back to her room, slamming her door. Moments later Jack heard the blast from her latest downloads thumping through the walls. Sally would be up any minute to make her turn it down. But as he listened, he could feel the difference between his boring twang noises and the angry energy that boomed out from Holly's room.

He picked his guitar up again. How was he going to tell Biddy that he couldn't go through with it? It might be better to take Paddywack down to the dogs' home after all. He smacked the sides of the guitar with his fist. It trembled and gave off a low whine of sound. He thumped it again. He strummed it fast. So fast, his fingers hurt. He played Nick Nack Paddywack angrily. Then he added in a few of his own made-up words.

Nick nack paddywack.
Your owner's never comin' back.

Louder. Faster. Jack was up on the bed. He had his head thrown back and his eyes shut. There were blisters on his fingers. His guitar seemed to be making music all on its own.

You was all that I had.
But you left me in a bag.
But you won't hear me cry
'cos I'm done with all your lies ...

... with a nick nack tough luck Jack.
Give a dog a bone.
Stick your kid in a foster home.

And somehow the song was about Paddywack, and somehow the song was about Dad. Jack's eyes were streaming, even though he never cried. And it didn't matter that he couldn't sing because he could rap in between Paddywack howling to the main tune.

The final clinch came when he stopped playing and opened his eyes.

Holly, Lucas and Max were all crowded in the doorway.

Lucas said, "Impressive."

Max said, "Can you do another one?"

Holly was just staring at him, her eyes angel-wide. "That's ... um ... OK." For once, she didn't sound fake.

And Jack knew what sort of act he could do for the talent show.

TALENT SPOTTERS

It was the day of the talent show.

"I'd better go." Jack hooked his guitar case over his shoulder and went into the hall. "We're ... er ... we're going off to visit that friend of Miss Biddle's today. Remember I told you about her?"

Sally was gazing at Jack as if he had a halo floating above his head. "I'm so very proud of you." She beamed as he opened the front door. "I'm sure Miss Biddle's friend will love your guitar playing. It's so kind of you to agree to go out and entertain her. You've been wonderful all summer."

Holly made vomit noises.

Lucas pulled a face. "I don't get how you can stand to go into old ladies' houses. They must stink."

"No more than you do. I think Jack's been wonderful too. Jack is awesome." Max grinned at Jack, and Jack high-fived him. Max glowed with happiness.

Jack was happy too – in a nervous way. Something had changed since that night they'd all watched his version of 'Nick Nack'. Holly and Lucas seemed OK with him, and even when they started on him, their comments were more like mates teasing each other. Max followed him around like a shadow. Jack almost wished he could have told them what he was doing. He had the feeling they'd be on his side.

"See you all later." Jack held a hand up to them all.

Biddy came out from her own house, carrying a brightly wrapped box. "A present for my dear friend, Valerie," she said loudly, winking at Jack and smiling at the others, who had all come out to wave them off.

Minutes later they were in Biddy's beetle-shaped car, driving towards the town hall. Jack tore the paper from the box, and Paddywack scrambled out. The puppy licked Jack's face and chewed his fingers. "Hey Pads, this is our big day," said Jack, scratching the puppy's ears.

"Look at that queue!" Biddy drove along the road that led past the town hall.

Jack nodded, taking in the hundreds of people

that lined the streets. "That's our competition." Jack held Paddywack up to the window as they went beyond the queue, heading further along the road looking for a place to park. Just then Jack saw someone. "Hey, I know that guy over by the pub. The one with the beard and the skinny dog."

"I can't look now. I'm driving."

Jack craned his neck but he couldn't get a proper look because there were people hanging round the pub doorway and they blocked his view, but just the thought of that beardy weirdy gave Jack goosebumps again.

A new thought jabbed at him. "What if someone we don't like wants to give Pads a home? Someone we don't trust?"

"We won't let them have him. Simple."

"But how we can be sure who's OK and who isn't? Maybe this isn't such a good idea?"

"You can't back out now. Not after all the hard work you've put in. And we can't keep poor Paddywack hidden for ever. I'm sure we'll find him that special home he deserves and I promise you that we'll stay in touch with whoever it is that takes him. We'll make sure he's always happy and well cared for."

Jack let himself relax. He was just having pre-performance nerves. Why would someone like Beardy Weirdy want Paddywack anyway? He didn't look like he could feed his own dog properly, let alone take on another one.

Biddy managed to squeeze her car into a gap between two vans and soon they were joining the end of the queue.

In front of them, a teenage girl was checking her long blonde hair in a hand mirror. A chubby guy in a leopard suit kept doing somersaults. A group of four younger girls huddled together, looking round at everyone and giggling.

The line shuffled forward. People were going in. Slowly. "They'll still be auditioning at midnight," Biddy sighed.

The blonde girl spoke without looking away from her mirror. "It's quicker than you think. They've got four lots of auditions going on at the same time, in different parts of the building. It's only if you pass your first auditions that you get to perform in front of the real judges and a proper audience."

"That's true." The leopard-suit guy stopped somersaulting and stroked Paddywack's head. "If you get through that bit, you get on the telly."

"Have you two done it before then?" said Biddy.

"Loads of times," said the girl.

"Every year since I was fourteen," said the leopard-suit guy. "I've got as far as performing in front of the judges, but I've never made it to the telly bit."

"Me neither." The girl wrinkled her nose and shrugged. "Maybe this year will be lucky for us both."

"Maybe. They've got Marcus Dowell on the judge's panel. And Pixie Pink, of course. The third judge is always the mayor." The leopard-suit guy somersaulted off again. The line shuffled forward.

They'd been right. The line did move fast. Within ten minutes Jack, Paddywack and Biddy were following a woman with a clipboard down a long carpeted corridor. She stopped by a carved wooden door and asked them their details, writing down notes.

Paddywack tried to chew the end of her pen.

"Wait here," sighed the woman, snatching her pen away. She opened the door and went in, then came out again. "You can go through now."

A skinny man with sticky-up hair was reading the notes on the clipboard. He looked up as they walked in. "Hello – er – Jack Jones? My name's

Ken. Fan*tastic* to see you." He glanced behind him at a woman with super bright red lipstick. "This one's for you, Hilary," he said. "Another musician."

"Just sit in that chair there." Hilary stifled a yawn. "I'm afraid your granny needs to leave. But if you get through, she can join the audience in the main hall this afternoon. Not the dog though, I'm afraid. Unless it's your granny's 'hearing dog' or something."

"Nothing wrong with my hearing." Biddy bristled as she turned to leave. "And the dog is part of Jack's act."

"Just says guitar and song here." Hilary tapped the clipboard with her bright red fingernail.

"Sorry," Jack said. "We must have filled in the form wrong." He saw Ken and Hilary exchange glances. They might as well have said *couple of idiots* out loud. "Shall I fill in a new one?"

This time Hilary did actually yawn. "No, no. We did just see another dog act. Not to our standards I'm afraid. The – er – gentleman became a trifle upset with us when we explained we couldn't put him and his dog through. I had to put out a call to security and get him taken away. His poor dog looked terrified. A skinny, brown thing. It looked hungry too." She sniffed loudly, as if the other dog-act had left a rotten smell in the room. "Let's hope you'll prove a bit easier to manage. Just do whatever you do." Hilary turned to Biddy. "I'm afraid you really *do* need to leave."

"I'm going." Biddy backed away, mouthing 'good luck' to Jack.

Jack set Paddywack down on the ground and sat on the chair. Paddywack perched neatly at Jack's feet. His head was on one side and he looked up at Jack, as if he was asking: *when we gonna start?*

Jack clicked his fingers. Paddywack trotted round the guitar case, gripped the zipper in his teeth and undid the zip. He opened the lid of the case with his muzzle. Then he barked twice.

"You want something?" Jack hoped he didn't sound too stilted.

Paddywack sniffed the guitar, and brushed the strings with his mouth, just enough so they gave off a soft musical twang.

"You want me to play?"

Paddywack sat up and begged.

Jack took the guitar out, and Paddywack stood wagging his tail, as if he was waiting for Jack to throw him a ball.

"OK, if you insist."

Jack strummed the chords, starting slowly. Paddywack swayed slightly, as if he was dancing. Jack played Nick Nack Paddywack gently. Paddywack lay down and whined softly in time to the music.

Hilary leant towards Ken and whispered, "How sweet."

Jack played faster. Paddywack sat up and yelped faster.

"Different," said Ken.

Suddenly Jack jumped up from the chair, pushing it over with a clatter.

Hilary gasped and leapt backwards as if she thought Jack was about to attack her.

You was all that I had.
But you left me in a bag.

Paddywack lifted his head, and howled.

But you won't hear me cry
'cos I'm done with all your lies ...

Jack span round on his heel. Paddywack bounced up and ran round with him. Jack faced Hilary and Ken, closing his eyes, strumming the beat and rapping out the last lines.

... with a nick nack tough luck Jack.
Give a dog a bone.
Stick your kid in a foster home.

Paddywack gave one last howl, then jumped inside the guitar case, pulling the lid down.

Jack opened his eyes, and nodded at Hilary and Ken. "Thank you very much for listening."

Hilary had tears streaming down her cheeks, and Ken started laughing and punching the air.

"What an act. Fan*tastic*. Both of you." Ken shook Jack's hand, then grinned at Hilary. "I think we might have discovered something at last."

Hilary wiped her tears, smudging her make-up and leaving patchy streaks across her face. "I think so too," she sniffed.

SHOW-STOPPER

Paddywack gave one last howl, then jumped inside the guitar case, pulling the lid down. Jack nodded his thanks at the audience, and then turned to the judges. "Thank you very much for listening." He opened the lid of the guitar case and Paddywack bounced out. They both bowed together. Jack picked Paddywack up.

The applause died down at last. The audience sat back in their seats. Jack scanned the room for Biddy. He knew she was there somewhere, but the stage lights had dazzled his eyes and he hadn't picked her out.

"Well, well, well." Marcus Dowell smiled. His teeth were a sparkling white. "I'm not keen on dog acts, but I've never seen – or perhaps I should say 'heard' – anything this good before. The guitar playing needs a bit of work but I have to say, it didn't seem to matter. You had this lot ..." he waved round at the audience, "... in the palm of your hand. What did you think, Pixie?"

"I *love* dog acts," Pixie gushed, "so I was ready to adore whatever you did. But that mix of guitar and 'doggie-song' – I mean, it was *sooo* beautiful. And funny. And clever. The two of you just blew me away."

"And you're a local boy?" The mayor was clearly impatient about having to wait to give an opinion. "Where do you live?"

"I'm only sort of local." Jack was still dazed by the lights, and the crowd. "I'm in a foster home. I used to live with my dad 'cos my mum died when I was small, but my dad sort of – well, I haven't seen him in a while." Jack didn't want to talk about the way Dad had dumped him, but no one seemed interested in Dad anyway.

"So you performed this for your mum? For her memory?" Pixie's eyes filled with tears. "That's *sooo* beautiful."

"Not really. I ..." Jack was stumbling over his words. The truth was he didn't really remember his mum all that well. "I found Paddywack in a plastic bag, and once I knew he could sing, I thought if people knew how clever he was it would help him find a new owner."

"A plastic bag?" Pixie was weeping openly now. The mayor kept patting her arm. "People are so *cruel*. But I bet all the little children at your foster home love Paddypaws."

"Paddywack. I've – er – had to keep him hidden. Sally wouldn't have let me keep him. She's the foster mum." Jack could see some of the audience dabbing their eyes with tissues. Some had their hands clamped over their mouths.

Pixie let out a small sob. "A foster mum with a heart of stone. That's an outrage. All those little children in her care, too." Pixie turned to the mayor. "That home should be investigated."

"No, you've got it wrong. Sally's OK. But the kids I live with aren't little children. Even Max is nearly eight. And we've all got problems. Sally does her best to keep us under control."

"What sort of problems?" Marcus Dowell drummed his fingers on the table, and leant forward.

"Just usual foster kid things." Jack felt as if he was drowning and had forgotten how to swim. He remembered something Biddy had said. "Being fostered can be tough. Harder than having a more every-day sort of home." He spoke in a rush, trying to explain that the others were OK, but that it was just difficult to live with strangers sometimes. "Lucas has been there the longest, and he was my mate for a while, but then he got bored with me. Then there's Max, who doesn't do that well at school and gets sent home a lot, but I totally get how that happens. I went through that when I was his age. It doesn't make him bad or anything. And Holly can be cross and bossy, but it was because of her and Lucas pushing me into a ditch that I found Paddywack."

There was a gasp from the audience.

"They pushed you into a ditch? What did your foster mother do about that?"

"She – er – I didn't tell her."

"Standard bully behaviour. They frighten their victims into keeping quiet." The mayor was making notes. "This all needs looking into."

"No, you don't get it. I need to try and explain better." Jack searched the audience again for Biddy and suddenly caught sight of her right at the back. She was being dragged away by a security guard.

Had she upset someone? There was no time to think it through, because hundreds of people were watching him and he had to try and make them understand. "It's OK at Sally's. We've all got stuff to deal with, that's all I meant. And I didn't come here to talk about any of that. Me and my neighbour Miss Biddle kept Paddywack a secret so he could get strong, and we could find him a good home. A home where he'd be special."

"Yes, yes." Pixie was smiling through a new wash of tears. "I can see that someone who has been through everything you've been through would want Paddypants to have a better start in life. We're all on your side, my darling. We can all feel your pain."

"I think we should vote." Marcus Dowell gleamed a smile at Jack. "Although I don't think there's any doubt about how it's going to go."

The audience cheered and roared as the three judges said 'yes'.

Jack stood blinking in the spotlight, knowing he'd messed things up.

Tragic Tale

The local paper dropped through the letterbox late the next afternoon. Paddywack's face gazed out at Jack.

TRAGIC TALE OF PLASTIC-BAG PUPPY.

SHAME ON 'HEART OF STONE' FOSTER-MUM WHO TURNED HER BACK ON A STARVING STRAY.

The report went on:

A CLAIM AGAINST CRUELTY WAS MADE YESTERDAY AT THE ANNUAL AUDITIONS FOR 'TALENT TIME.'

Jack Jones stole the show with singing dog sensation 'Paddynack' – the judges were amazed at the talent and both dog and boy received a standing ovation.

But the glory was tainted by Jack's account of the cruelty at his foster home. The audience heard how the foster mother, Sally Charm, had ignored bullying and abuse in the home.

Knowing the puppy would suffer at the hands of Sally Charm, talented rap artist Jack trained the puppy in secret. His efforts were rewarded – all three judges voted them though to final.

In a later interview the mayor, Harry Valiant, promised to investigate conditions at the home.

Yesterday, when they drove home, Biddy had been keen to go round and talk to Sally and explain everything but Jack begged her not to. He'd had a vague hope that everyone would forget the whole thing once they'd gone home, and he hadn't even realised there was a newspaper reporter in the room. What an idiot he was. But maybe there was still a chance he could keep things hidden from Sally and the others – at least until Paddywack was safely in some new home with new owners. Surely someone would come forward soon?

Luckily, everyone was out. Shoving the newspaper under his T-shirt, Jack raced outside. He scrambled across the fence into Biddy's garden and sprinted round the back of the shed. Then he tore the newspaper into shreds.

"Jack? Are you all right?" Biddy came out as Jack walked up to her house. She had Paddywack in her arms.

Jack took him from Biddy. "The free paper just came. It says loads of bad stuff. I've trashed it." Jack held Paddywack tightly. The idea of Sally reading that front page made him sick with guilt. And what would Holly and Lucas do? He'd be more dead than the dinosaurs if they saw what the paper had printed.

"I've just read the paper too." Biddy sighed. "But just getting rid of one copy won't help much. Everyone round here gets that free paper. We can't wait any longer. Even if Sally doesn't read the report herself she's going to hear about it from someone else. We need to talk to her before that

TRAGIC TALE

do-gooder mayor starts causing trouble."

"We?"

"I can explain better than you. I know how much they've twisted your words. It's disgusting. I was furious at the time – remember I told you the security guard made me leave because I tried to get nearer the stage?"

Jack nodded. Biddy had said they'd been playing cheap games with him, just to give the audience a bit of a 'sob-story'. "What about Pads? Everyone will want to know where I kept him, and when they find out you've been part of it, the landlord might kick you out of your house."

"I'm sure it won't come to that." Biddy sounded fierce, but when Jack glanced at her, her face seemed pale. "But I was just coming to pop Paddywack in the shed before I talk to Sally. I don't want any reporters discovering where he lives. They'd only want more heartbreak pictures. Although, I'm sure people will be begging to own him now. So at least that's been a success."

"Yeah. That's one good thing," Jack said miserably. So this was how it would all end. The foster home would be closed down. Everyone would hate him for ever. And he'd never see

Paddywack again.

They put Paddywack in the shed. "He'll be fine for half an hour." Biddy smiled at Jack. "I'm sure I won't be out longer than that. Sally's an angel of a person. She'll understand everything."

"*She* might," Jack muttered. "But the others won't." He trudged up the path with Biddy, following her through the house and out the front door. She opened her gate, about to head round into Jack's house to see if Sally was back yet.

Then, three things happened.

A police car drew up.

Holly and Lucas came down the street.

And a bearded man tapped Biddy on the shoulder. "'Scuse me," he waved the newspaper article in her face, "but I'm looking for this Jack Jones bit of scum. The pup in the picture 'aint his. He nicked it from me. I train dogs to do tricks for entertainment type acts and I'd just started work on it when it went missing."

Jack didn't hear what Biddy said. He was edging towards her front door again. He only had seconds to make his escape.

THIRD TIME UNLUCKY

Jack snuck out of Miss Biddy's shed, ran down the garden and scrambled over the rickety fence at the back. "We need to get away from traffic and houses and people," he told Paddywack. "I'm not sure how much time we've got. We'll head for the park."

Paddywack's ears bounced and his nose twitched as he took in all the new smells.

The park was quiet. A few younger kids were kicking a ball about, but they were a long way off. Jack slowed to a walk, gasping for breath and with a stitch in his side. "Think we'll head along by the ditch," he puffed. "I doubt those kids will have seen that newspaper, but the less people who catch sight of us, the better."

The ditch was still stinky, although it wasn't so soggy as before because it hadn't rained much all summer. The trolley was still there. The plastic bag lay scrunched in the bottom. "This is where we first met," Jack whispered to Paddywack. He felt a twist in his gut when he thought about what would have happened if he hadn't tried to get that rat out of the bag.

"Finding you is the best thing I've done. Ever," Jack said. "I don't care how much trouble I get in. I'm going to keep looking out for you until I come up with someone decent to hand you over to." The dogs' home was his only hope now. He had to find one before Beardy Weirdy caught up with him.

He reached the meshed wire fence by the building site. There were KEEP OUT signs everywhere. He could see men in hard hats standing around by a big yellow digger. "What d'you think, Pads?" Jack murmured. "We either creep through there, or go back onto the main road? You up for a risk?"

Paddywack whimpered and licked Jack's nose. "Get off, slobber-chops," Jack grinned. "I'll take that as a 'yes'. I'll have to climb this fence one-handed, but I won't drop you. Promise."

Moments later, Jack and Paddywack were inside the site. Jack set off in the opposite direction to the builders in hats. "Those houses there are still being built, but at least their roofs are on," he told Paddywack. "We can hide in one while I think what to do." He started to jog again, and glanced down at Paddywack, but though his ears were still bouncing, the puppy's eyes were tight shut. He'd gone to sleep.

They reached the half-built houses and Jack crossed the mud patches that would be gardens one day. The first two houses had doors and windows fitted. He knew there must be security cameras nearby; it was too risky to try to break in.

"There – it's our lucky day. The builders haven't got as far as doors and windows with that third place." Jack glanced behind him. Everything was quiet. Very still. Jack walked up to the doorway and stepped into the hall. It smelt of brick and plaster and cement. The walls were an ugly grey breeze-block.

Suddenly the fur on Paddywack's back bristled. Jack tensed up. "What's the ...?" he started, but he didn't finish.

A black beast of a dog came hurtling out from deep inside the house. It stopped just paces in front of them. It snarled, its eyes fixed on Jack with a dead, killer stare.

Jack pressed against the wall. Beastdog growled, an ugly rumble that seemed to come more from its gut than its throat. It had a metal chain clipped to its studded collar, and Jack realised the only reason it wasn't ripping him and Paddywack to pieces was because it was tied up.

Still, that chain might break.

"Time to go," Jack muttered. He edged away. Beastdog tried to leap after them. It snapped its jaws. Saliva frothed up in its mouth. The chain stretched so tight it made Beastdog gag.

A gruff voice from the back of the house shouted, "What's up, Brutus? It better not be those kids again."

The sound of heavy footsteps echoed from the room Beastdog had sprung from. A man appeared. Jack took in that he was chubby and wearing a black uniform. He looked straight at Jack and his eyes held that same killer stare.

CHAIN REACTION

"Stop! STOP! It'll be worse for you if I have to chase after you!"

Jack's feet pounded as he sprinted away. He knew Paddywack must be being jolted and shaken, but he couldn't let Beastdog or his zombie-eyed owner catch them.

Racing towards the far end of the building site, Jack crashed through nettles and brambles.

An old ivy covered wall ran along the length of the site, and beyond that Jack could see more houses. Proper finished houses that people already lived in. A wall would be harder to climb than a mesh fence, but there was no choice. At least the ivy would be good for footholds. "Here we go, Pads. Up, up and away." Gripping the ivy with one hand, and pressing Paddywack tight to his chest with the other, Jack scrambled up. He could hear Beastdog snarling. A moment later it was beneath them. Its frenzied paws tore at the ivy. Its chain rattled against the bricks as it hurled itself up again and again.

Jack scrabbled higher. The ivy was thinner here. Would it hold his weight? His knuckles were grazed and bleeding. He couldn't hold on much longer and the ivy was ripping away from the brickwork. Glancing back, Jack saw Beastdog with its muzzle raised and its jaws open. Ready for the kill.

Jack gave one final push and made it to the top of the wall. He straddled it, shifting his hold on Paddywack to get a better grip. They were both trembling. It was a long drop down and the ivy had been stripped away on the other side. There was nothing to hold onto.

Paddywack licked Jack's nose and whimpered.

Zombie-eyes appeared, puffing and wheezing. "You won't get away this time. I'm sick of you kids causing trouble. I've already alerted the police." He jerked the chain and Beastdog gagged and strained sideways, still not taking its eyes off Jack. "You come down or I'll let go of him. He's trained to kill. No messing. There's no one around to know he didn't just get away from me. I'll say I tried my best to hold him off you ..."

Jack realised he was a security guard. It didn't seem likely he'd climb the wall himself, but if he let go of Beastdog's chain then it would be 'game over'.

Jack looked down at the garden below. "This isn't the time for wimping out, Jack Jones," he muttered between clenched teeth. "OK, Pads. Flying lesson number one."

Jack swung his leg over so he was sitting sideways on the wall. He closed his eyes. "This is gonna *huurt*," he sang, as he leapt.

It didn't hurt. Not much, anyway. They landed on a mound of soft earth. "Phew. Miracles can happen." Jack blew a kiss into the dusky sky, then scrambled up, brushing mud from his hair and face. He looked back up at the wall, waiting to see Beastdog's head appear as it scrabbled over the top to get them, but although he could still hear frenzied barking, nothing happened.

"No time to rest though; if that guard's really called the police they'll be here any minute." Jack stumbled on. And then he stopped. He'd seen those roses round those patio doors before. "Another miracle, Pads."

This was Emily's garden. Emily was still away. And Jack knew where they kept a spare key.

TROUBLE BUBBLE

Jack kicked off his trainers just inside the patio doors, but he was still trailing mud as he carried Paddywack through to the kitchen. "You thirsty, Pads?" He found a bowl to fill with water. Paddywack lapped it up, then widdled on the floor.

"Cheers," Jack laughed. He found a cloth under the sink and mopped up the puddle. "You need a litter tray, don't you? I'll use a cooking dish and stick paper in it."

He knew if Emily were here, she'd be up for helping him. Emily's mum and dad probably doted on their only daughter, so they'd forgive him in the end. Wouldn't they?

Jack's gut was rumbling. "It's got to be past dinner time, Pads. I'm starved." He hunted through the cupboard. "Beans." He was relieved that even Emily's posh-toff parents had normal food. "For me, not you. I'll find something else for you."

The freezer was stuffed full of fish and meat and Jack took out a bag of organic chicken breasts. "I'll thaw a couple in the microwave, then we can feast. Beans. Chicken. And – cool – look - microwave chips."

Half an hour later they'd eaten and Jack was thinking how perhaps Emily would let him hide here forever? There'd been this girl in Holland – Anne Frank – who'd managed that for two years in a war. He remembered learning about her in his old school.

"That might be good for me, but not for you, Pads. You need a decent home where you don't have to be a secret any more." Jack bent and ruffled Paddywack's ears. "There's a laptop in Emily's room. It's a girly pink colour and I made fun of it when I was here. As long as she hasn't taken it on holiday, I can google dog rescue places. Then all I have to do is find a way to get you there."

Jack reached the stairs. Paddywack bounded past him, racing to the top and then rushing down again, as if it was all some new and wonderful game.

Evening was drawing in and the landing at the top looked gloomy, but Jack didn't dare put on the lights. He was sure the neighbours would be keeping an eye on the place for Emily's family. "Hope you're not scared of the dark, Pads," he said.

Paddywack raced up and down the stairs again, going so fast he tumbled the last few steps.

"That'll teach you," laughed Jack.

Paddywack barked and wagged his tail, then raced up to the top again.

The landing was full of shadows. The bedroom doors were all closed and Jack's feet made no sound as he walked across the plush carpet to the one he thought was Emily's.

Opening the door, he peered in at a lilac bedspread. "Result! Emily's laptop's here too. Right there on the table by her bed."

Paddywack dodged past him into the room, grabbing a purple fluffy slipper from under the bed and shaking it.

"Easy, Pads. They'll probably make me pay for all breakages." Jack made a grab for the slipper but Paddywack bounced backward, a puppy growl rumbling in his throat.

Bits of purple fluff floated down onto the carpet. "OK, you're testing your teeth. I give up."

Jack turned the laptop on.

The light from the screen flickered blue. He put it on the floor and lay on his front, waiting for it to load up.

The motor whirred. The screensaver came on. It was a kitten with false teeth, which might have been cute if Jack had had time to look at it.

Where was the internet icon? What if he needed a password to get in?

And then Jack's heart nearly exploded in his chest. Noises burst out all round him. Someone was shouting. Jack leapt up, kicking the laptop in his panic. The lead pulled out with a twist; it looked broken.

The voice filled the room, almost vibrating the walls it was so loud.

Paddywack dropped the purple slipper, sprang onto the bed and tilted his head.

The shouting turned into a song.

Jack slumped down on the bed beside Paddywack, sagging with relief. "It's Pixie Pink. Emily must have set it up on her laptop." Paddywack sniffed his neck, then sat on his head.

"Gerroff. I don't want your bum on my face." Jack laughed, pushing the puppy away and sitting up.

Paddywack sat up too, tilting his head again.

Pixie Pink screamed out: *You're just trouble. Burstin' bubbles.*

Paddywack whined. He barked. He howled in time to the tune.

Jack ruffled his head. "You could do your doggy-songs to anything." Relief that nothing bad was happening made him laugh so hard that his side ached. A moment later he started howling too, yelping along with Paddywack. The false teeth kitten stared out from the laptop.

Pixie Pink screeched: *Did ya think I was rough and tough?* Jack stood up on the bed, bounced, then jumped off. *Couldn't ya see I'd had enough?* He stomped his feet. He moshed.

Paddywack joined in, bouncing and leaping. They both howled and whined and yelped. Jack picked the puppy up, spinning and hopping. And then, he felt something wet on his hands.

"Not again." He looked down at the damp patch on Emily's cream carpet.

Pixie Pink sang: *So goodbye, and don't cry 'cos I'll*

know it's all a lie.

"I forgot to sort that litter tray. You widdled again." Jack wiped his hands on Emily's quilt and then felt bad about it. He'd have to own up to that at some point. In fact, he'd have to own up to loads of things. There was mud and mess everywhere downstairs. He'd nicked a load of food. He'd broken Emily's precious pink laptop.

Things were going to get rough and tough sometime very soon.

Pixie Pink paused between songs.

In the sudden silence, Jack heard footsteps on the stairs.

The trouble bubble was most definitely about to burst.

ALL CHANGE

It was Sally who spoke first. "Jack. We've been so worried. The neighbours heard barking in here, and it wasn't rocket science to realise it was you. Especially when I knew it was Emily's house."

Two policemen stood behind her in the doorway. Jack hugged Paddywack.

"We will have to take a statement. This still counts as breaking and entering," said the first policeman, switching the light on and striding over to the laptop. He lifted it up, squinting at the cable. Pixie Pink launched into something about how some bad boy had *stole my sunshine.*

The policeman closed the laptop, shutting off Pixie Pink.

Paddywack whined and Jack hugged him tighter.

"We know why you did it," Sally said gently. "Miss Biddle told us everything."

"What are you going to do with me?"

The second policeman made his lips into a thin line. "As my partner has just said, we'll take a statement. It will be up to the house owners as to whether they press charges. It might depend on how much mess you've made. And – er – how much damage you've done." He looked at the damp patch on the carpet, the laptop that was now back on the table, and the chewed up purple slipper.

Jack faced the three of them. Paddywack squirmed in his arms. He kept wagging his tail, as if the three new visitors were some sort of surprise party just for him. "You can't give Pads back to that guy with the beard. His other dog was terrified of him. I want Pads to have a special home with special people." The tears were streaming down Jack's face, and he wiped them away with the back of his hand. "That's all it was ever about."

Sally put a hand on Jack's arm. "Miss Biddle knew that bearded man from a long time ago, when she used to train dogs for television. Apparently he got sacked for not feeding the dogs he was looking after. She's contacted a dog-watch warden who is going to check out why his current dog is so thin and scared, and if he's found guilty of cruelty he could be banned from ever keeping a dog again. And even if he's not, he won't come after Paddywack. He won't want to draw extra attention to himself."

Jack sniffed loudly. "Are you in trouble because of me? The things they said in the newspaper?"

"No, silly. Social Services know what the newspapers are like. I've been fostering for years and I'm checked up on regularly. There's nothing to worry about."

"What about Pads then? What'll happen to him?"

"He's coming back with us for the moment, to Miss Biddle's. Holly's sat with her now. She can't wait to see the puppy everyone's talking about."

"Just the puppy?" Jack sniffed. "I bet she won't want to see me."

"Well, knowing Holly, I doubt she'll show it, but 'awesome' is the word she used to describe you."

"Awesome?" Jack nearly dropped Paddywack onto the policeman's foot. "Holly said I was awesome?"

STAR TURN

"Jack and Paddysnack. How *fabulous* to see you both again." Pixie Pink gleamed out a smile.

Jack gave a small bow and Paddywack sat neatly beside the guitar case, his head tilted, ready to start.

Marcus Dowell glanced down at his notes. "Ah, yes. The singing dog. I remember your local audition. What are you doing for us today?"

"It's the same song as last time, but I think my guitar playing might have improved. I've been having extra lessons." Jack gave a nod to the audience, hoping to spot Mr Chung but the stage lights were too dazzling. He couldn't pick anyone out.

"Excellent. We've got some very strong acts this year – including a dancing donkey. That one is my favourite so far." Marcus Dowell leant back in his chair and put his hands behind his head.

"Oooh yes, the dancing donkey is *delicious*." Pixie Pink closed her eyes and gave a little wiggle of her shoulders, as if she were being stroked by the memory.

Jack had seen the dancing donkey. There was also a boy who could do awesome acrobatics and a school choir who sang so beautifully the whole audience had wept. Jack couldn't see that he and Paddywack stood much chance but that didn't matter. Biddy already had a list of people who had come forward from the last audition, all of them wanting to give Paddywack that 'special home'. She'd turned them all down. She'd got permission from the landlord to keep a dog on a 'temporary basis' and when Jack asked her how long that meant, she'd told him not to worry. So Jack wasn't worrying. He trusted Biddy. And maybe today that special person would watch this act and fall in love with Paddywack and it would all be sorted at last.

"Go for it, Jack," Holly yelled from somewhere over to the left of the stalls.

Someone near her – probably Lucas – gave a wild whoop.

"When you're ready," said Chaz Chester, the third judge.

Jack clicked his fingers. Paddywack trotted round the guitar case, gripped the zipper in his teeth and undid the zip.

TALE END

"Budge up. You're taking up half the sofa." Holly plonked herself down next to Jack and Emily.

Max rolled on Biddy's front-room floor, giggling, while Paddywack sniffed his feet.

Sally came in carrying a tray of drinks, and Biddy followed her. "I hope you all like popcorn. I've made a big pile."

"It's an incredible kitchen Biddy's got here." Sally smiled round at everyone. "The whole house is a dream."

Biddy beamed as she put the popcorn down on the table and sat in the chair opposite. "It *is* a dream house and it's so wonderful to be living in the countryside again. The bluebells are out at the moment and everywhere is so charming. But I'm just so very happy to be working with dogs again. It's one job you never get too old for."

"You must earn masses, Biddy," said Holly, grabbing a handful of popcorn. "This place must cost you loads."

"Holly!" said Sally. "That's not a very polite thing to say." She sat next to Biddy, a cake in one hand and a cup of tea balanced on her knee.

"Oh, I don't mind." Biddy smiled at Holly. "The house comes with the kennels here, so I don't pay rent. But you're right, the film companies do pay well. It's all thanks to Jack. If he hadn't got all that publicity from coming third in the talent show my old boss would never have got in touch, Paddywack would never have got the role in the film, and I wouldn't have been offered this top training job. I've got much to thank you for, Jack."

Jack felt his cheeks burn, but Holly leant across Emily and poked his chest. "Don't get big-headed. You're still annoying sometimes."

"Only sometimes?" Jack grinned at her.

"Well, OK. Most times." Holly and Emily said this together, then looked at each other and laughed.

Jack grinned again. They weren't exactly like a

family at the foster home, but they all got on most of the time. It felt good. Dad had made contact since the televised show and that felt good too but Jack wasn't holding his breath on that one. The truth was, even if Dad suddenly begged Jack to live with him again, he wasn't sure he'd want to go. As long as they met up regularly – and Dad had promised he wouldn't let Jack down again – then that felt like enough for now.

Added to all of that, nothing bad had happened about breaking into Emily's house last year. In fact, she insisted he *hadn't* broken in. She had, after all, shown him where the key was. Their cleaner sorted the mess. Her dad fixed the laptop cable, and her mum bought her a kitten. Jack had never worked out the connection with the kitten bit, but it was something to do with her mum not having realised Emily was into animals, and a cat was better than a dog because they went abroad so much.

Lucas looked up from the DVD player he'd been fussing with. "Ready for me to start?" he said.

"Ready," they all said together.

The film began.

The title stretched across the screen.

PA🐾PRINT PRODUCTIONS

P R E S E N T S

ROCK DOGZ
THE MUSICAL

And there was Paddywack on a sunbed, stretched out beside a pool at a luxury villa.

"Cool combo." Lucas reached for a handful of popcorn. "It's real footage mixed with animation. Awesome sunglasses."

"Sweet," breathed Holly and Emily together.

Then Emily added, "Are they Pixie Pink's legs in the background? Walking across the garden? I can't wait for the bit where her and Paddywack sing together."

"That's not till halfway through," said Jack. "It was the scene I saw get filmed. They were shooting it that day they interviewed me for the back story bit."

"We know." Holly gave a fake yawn. "You've only told us ten billion times."

"I can't believe you actually hung out with Pixie Pink. She gave you her milkshake."

"Thirsty work, getting interviewed," Jack grinned.

"Shhh," grumbled Max, sitting up. Paddywack stopped sniffing his feet and sat next to him. "I can't hear."

"No one's said anything yet." Lucas rolled his eyes.

But everyone was smiling.

"Awesome." Holly was biting her knuckles, her eyes fixed on the screen.

Paddywack tilted his head at the screen for a moment, then yawned. Turning, he trotted over to Jack, settled down at his feet, and fell asleep.

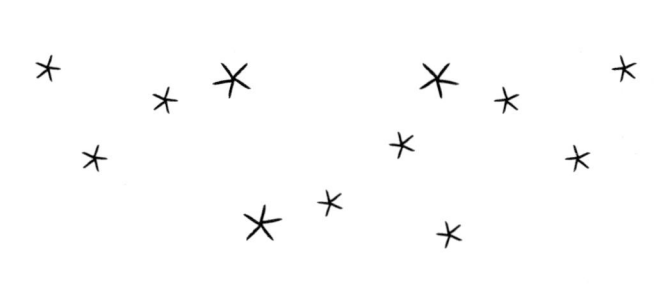

WORDTAMER CREATIVE WRITING:
TIPS AND TRICKS

ANIMAL ANTICS

Some stories are inspired by real events, and real people. Pup Idol began after watching a dog win a television talent show. I created the dog first – a lost brown and white puppy – and then gave him a secret talent.

Try writing like this yourself.

Choose an animal. Dog? Horse? Lion? Snail? Something else?

Choose their secret talent. Singing? Dancing? Mind-Reading? Something else?

Where does that animal live? House? Forest? Jungle? Beach? Somewhere else?

Is there a 'good guy' who will discover your animal's talent? Children? Teenagers? Adults? Someone (or something) else?

Where will they hide the animal? Indoors? Outside? In a cave? Under the ground? Somewhere else?

Bring on the 'bad guy'. Create someone who wants to cause trouble. Boy? Girl? Man? Woman? Animal? Zombie? Something else? Think about what they look like. What do they want to do with it?

Your animal is lost. In your first paragraph, someone is going to find it. Is it someone good, or bad? Where will they find the animal? What will they do with it?

All of the above is to help you start thinking. If you suddenly come up with some new twist, or a different beginning, that's fine. It's normal for authors to experiment with possibilities and to change their minds about details as the idea gets stronger.

START WRITING YOUR STORY.

For more tips and tricks go to: www.wordtamer.co.uk

WORDTAMER *QUICK WORDS* SERIES:
another bite-sized story for you to feast on.

SCARE BEAR

JUDY WAITE

BODY SNATCHER

"I'm not into clowns." Jess tipped her bag of popcorn upside down. She shook the dregs onto the palm of her hand, then licked them off. "That one over there keeps watching us. Look."

Frankie glanced at where a clown stood by a roller-coaster ride. The words:

TUNNEL OF DOOM

dripped like blood across the entrance. The afternoon sunlight glinted on a black and silver train that waited on the tracks.

"Come and scare yourselves silly." The clown beckoned with a white-gloved hand. His painted lips looked like a freaky red sausage.

"No way am I going near him. He's seriously weird," muttered Jess.

"Shhh, he'll hear you." Frankie looked at the clown again. He had electric shock hair, all stuck up and spiky. Beside him, the tunnel of doom yawned like a dark mouth. Screaming skulls and body parts were painted all round the edge.

The clown's sausage mouth stretched into an ugly smile. "It'll be a ride you'll never forget. Only one token each."

"We – er – we didn't buy any tokens." Frankie made a show of shrugging, pushing his hands into his jeans' pocket to pretend they were empty. And then he stopped. His pockets *were* empty.

"What's up? You've gone whiter than that clown's face." Jess frowned.

Frankie felt panic prickle through him. "That cash I saved to get Meg's present. It's gone."

"Check again."

Frankie wiggled his finger into his jean's pocket again, this time feeling the gap in the bottom seam. "There's a hole."

Jess scrunched her empty popcorn container up and dropped it in a nearby bin. "In that case, it's fallen out in this park somewhere. We'll walk back round the fair. It might be on the grass."

"Who you kidding? Someone will have picked it up by now." Frankie knew Meg would wake at some stupid hour tomorrow and bounce into his room, all full of six-year-old birthday buzz. She'd find out he hadn't bought her that ballerina doll. The one she'd seen in the new shopping centre. He'd promised to get it and now he'd messed up. Again.

Jess's excited squeal broke into his thoughts. She bent and picked something up. "Awesome! Look. I've found a fairground token."

"What use is that? Maybe you think I should scare my sister silly by taking her into the tunnel of doom?"

"I don't s'pose Meg will be into splattered body parts, but there are other rides. What about the carousel? Or those giant tea-cups that you sit in?"

Frankie shook his head miserably. "She's been dreaming of that doll. It's going to be a massive let-down."

Jess put her hand on Frankie's arm and dragged him back a few paces. "Let's get away from here anyway. That clown's still watching us. He's creeping me out. We can use the token on that duck-grab thing back there. The prizes are cute cuddly teddies. If you win one of those, you could give that to Meg."

"*If* I won."

"Stop being such a grump. You can at least make an effort. Come on."

Frankie trudged behind her, all the way to the duck-grab.

A tubby man was busy fixing something with a screwdriver, but he put it down as they went closer. "Want to try your luck? Three chances to win."

"You bet." Jess held out the token. "Go for it, Frankie."

Frankie looked at the bears that lined the shelf at the back of the stall. They seemed OK. Meg would think they were cute. He stepped forward, even though he was sure he'd make an idiot of himself.

"You steer the claw with the arrows and press that middle button when you're ready to grab." The man's chubby cheeks puffed out as he talked. He had small, round eyes and a stubbled brown beard. He looked a bit like a bear himself. "It's easy as peasy. You just have to time it right," he said.

Frankie steered the claw. Left a bit. Right a bit. The toy ducks floated by, bobbing and quacking.

"It's cool those ducks can actually quack," said Jess.

"Don't distract your friend," the tubby man warned.

Frankie could tell that the man didn't think he stood a chance. He pressed the button. The claw made its grab seconds after the next duck had gone quacking by.

"Oopsy woopsy." The man was messing about with his screwdriver again, but he squinted up at Frankie. "Two more tries."

This time Frankie took it more slowly. He'd go for the third duck in the row. "Just keep calm," he muttered to himself.

"Oopsy woopsy, missed again," chuckled the man. "Just one last go."

Frankie wished he could lower a claw down and lift the man up. He'd make it take him away, high into the sky. Frankie pictured his chubby legs waving about as he went higher and higher, shouting his stupid oopsy woopsies to the clouds.

He took a deep breath. Getting hacked off with Mr Oopsy Woopsy wasn't going to help. But his hands were shaking. This mattered too much.

He looked at the bobbing yellow ducks again. "I can't do it." Frankie turned to Jess, holding his hand out for her to see how shaky he was.

"Try counting to ten. To calm down."

Frankie knew counting to ten wouldn't help. Not ten, nor twenty, nor even a hundred. "Will you do it?"

"I won't be any better than you." Jess held her own hand out. It stayed steady and still.

"Please," Frankie begged. "You won't make a bigger mess of it than me."

"Having a spot of troubly bubbly?" asked the man.

Jess looked at Frankie, and he could see she was trying to stop herself giggling. He'd have laughed too, if he'd been in a better mood.

"Say pleasy weezy," said Jess to Frankie.

"Don't push your lucky wucky."

"Go on – or we'll just have to go homey womey." Jess grinned.

Frankie rolled his eyes. "OK. You win. Pleasy weezy Jessy Wessy."

Jess punched him lightly on the shoulder. "My pleasure, Grumpy Wumpy." She nudged Frankie out of the way, and stood in front of the game. The ducks came round again, quacking and bobbing like before. Jess lowered the claw. Stopped. Waited. Then she lowered the claw again. She was going to miss. She wasn't quite in the right place.

"I can't look. This whole idea is doomed," Frankie muttered, turning away. And then he saw something ... it was a fluffy brown teddy bear, sat on its own at the side of the stall. Just an arm's length away.

The bear had yellow glass eyes that glittered strangely in the sunlight. Its nose was black plastic. Its mouth had been sewn with black cotton. The stitching was wonky, making the mouth turn downwards as if the bear was cross. It didn't seem like the friendliest bear in the world, but surely it was better than no bear at all?

If Frankie had thought it through, he wouldn't have done it. He never went looking for trouble. But Frankie didn't think it through. He stretched out his hand, closed his fingers round the bear's brown fluffy body, and snatched it.

WORDTAMER *QUICK WORDS* SERIES

for readers age 8 -14 years.

House of Secrets   **Pup Idol**   *Scare Bear*

FOR A LONGER READ:

Wordtamer Novel for readers aged 9 – 14 years.
Funfear

A quick word from the wordtamer. "All wordtamer books and the wordtamer website connect up characters, places and storylines."
www.wordtamer.co.uk

Lightning Source UK Ltd.
Milton Keynes UK
UKOW03f2021190614

233757UK00001B/1/P